HONEYMOON
IN
OVERDRIVE

A Tale of Love, Music, and Horsepower

I0537446

SUPERCHARGED PHOTO EDITION

DANNY O'TOOLE
www.OverdrivePress.com

▼

We want you to turn others on to this book and its e-book counterpart, but please respect and support the hard work of the indie author. Thank you.

Cover design, interior design, and photography by Danny O'Toole, Overdrive Press

Illustration and production by Angela O'Toole, Overdrive Press.

Copyright © 2014 by Danny O'Toole. All rights reserved. No part of this publication may be reproduced, stored in a retrieval system, or transmitted in any form or by any means, electronic, mechanical, photocopying, recording, or otherwise without the prior written permission of the copyright holder, except brief quotations used in a review. Contact the publisher for permission requests.

"Eiffel Tower and the Moon" ©2010-2013 by Leonel H. Ocampo, http://leocampo.deviantart.com. Used by permission.

This is a work of fiction. Names, characters, businesses, events, incidents, and places are either the products of the author's untamed imagination or used in a fictitious manner. Any resemblance to actual persons, living or dead, or real occurrences is purely coincidental.

NOTICE: This book includes sexually explicit material that is inappropriate for younger readers.

Published by
Overdrive Press
www.OverdrivePress.com

Additional information and discussion at
www.WriteYourSexyStory.com

*Dedicated to every young lover about to pop
the clutch*

HONEYMOON IN *OVERDRIVE*
By Danny O'Toole
www.OverdrivePress.com

CONTENTS

PART I: THE *COUP*

That's what I get for driving six hundred miles? 1
He had pledged himself to another 4
Motel Masochism 6
She had acted scandalized 7
Tonsils like that get you anything you want 10
Guitar God's gift to picky men 13

PART II: THE *COUPÉ*

Dazed and confused 17
Enjoy the show 19
A dish dished up for hungry eyes 21
Well, well, hello there 23
His mouth went dry 27
She sidled her gooey tart 28
A message any fool could decode 31
Wild West surrender 32

DEAR READER
FOR THE WRITER IN YOU
ACKNOWLEDGMENTS
WAIT, THERE'S MORE!
PHOTO ALBUM

The Author 42
The Hot Dish 43
The Martins 44
The Flower 45
The *Coup de l'Amour* 46

The Holley Trinity 47
The Big Apple 48
The Hat 49
What's In Store 50

PART I: THE *COUP*

"AH, YES. Your subtle expectations of married life." Angela shook her head and swatted him with the handcuffs.

"Ouch," Daniel said. "That's what I get for driving six hundred miles to ravish—I mean, lavish—my favorite fiancée with not one, but two surprise wedding presents? Maybe I'll hang onto the other one." He swept the Main Event, his *Coup de l'Amour*, behind his back. Never mind that in his fervor to get it to her the once-in-a-lifetime splurge had landed him, and his *Coupé de l'Ford*, before an Iowa kangaroo court of gun-wielding thugs—and that he still had to hustle his AWOL-weekend butt from her Minnesota bed back to his Illinois base before Monday's heartless reveille.

Ungrateful little snip. Let her dangle awhile.

He crossed his arms and squared out his chin. "I'll have you know those cuffs aren't just any, uh, testament to the bonds of matrimony. They're Lash LaRue specials I got for my seventh birthday, along with a Roy Rogers twin holster set. Then there's my Gene Autry Lil' Wrangler chaps and vest—which, by the by, I might not mind seeing you in." He drummed his biceps with deliberating fingers and eyeballed her from head to foot. "Yup. Either of them. You can pick."

She swatted him again. "More likely you'd not mind seeing any and all 'bonds of matrimony' serve up your 'favorite fiancée' in just the hat."

"For the love of—I'm glad those things are pint-sized! And how did you—that is—Wait, you little trickster, the word 'hat' never left my lips!

But if by chance that *is* the, um, 'outfit' I would like you in, Miss Know-it-all, what hat would it be?"

"Garsh, what consharned hat could it poshibly be?" she said, her lips curled in and eyes squinched.

"It is *not* a Gabby Hayes hat, dadgumit. And thankfully, young whippersnapper, yer fine visage makes yer impersonation plumb pathetic. But how in tarnation did yew know which hat I meant? And how did you get me talking like some grizzled, doddering, over-the-mesa forty-year-old? Anyway, I admit it has similar, er, character, but only because I wore it to a pulp as a kid. The fact is, I've never seen another like it."

It was true. No cowboy he'd ever heard of wore an emerald green hat. He got it on the same birthday as the white holster set with red spangles and the Autry attire, dark rust with yellow bucking bronco. The hat's soft felt fit him from the first day, when everything else was stiff and awkward. Envious friends tried to take it from him, but he held on tight. His Gabby-esque hat had served him well. Particularly, he thought with fresh stirrings, after Miss Adventurous moved it to the adult toy box—that trove of titillation she had so waggishly christened her "tail box." Yessiree, "Gabby" had amused and amazed ever since with what could be pulled out of an old green hat.

"I can't help it the very best comes to me in emerald green," he sniffed. "It's been my good luck color all my lucky twenty-six years. Fastest gun in grade school. Fastest car when stop turns to go. Then, of course, there's you." He ran his hand up her arm to the nape of her neck.

She yipped and raised the cuffs again, but he caught them overhead and applied mouth-to-mouth re-inclination.

"Mmmmph," she said, and stuck to him. Lip magnets, she called them.

He backed off from her happy pucker. He was up for plenty of pucking, but no more fooling around for now. He had rolled in at dawn to get his biscuit rolling done, and—to his ever-rolling dismay—would have to roll back out tomorrow night. But every grueling mile to and from the proverbial pallet she had made for him on the floor was worth it to pull off a bonus-filled weekend she would never forget. He fingered the hard-earned gift behind him, and his heart clambered LaRue-like into his throat. How many times had they fantasized about this great adventure? Shared wish lists? Discussed what to explore first? Someday, they told each other. Someday.

Well, good thing she's on the floor already! After his discovery last year he had often pictured how this bombshell moment would go. She would tear into the little green box with its bright red ribbon and big silver bow. Flip through its contents. Look up, astonished, adoring.

No need to worry what she would think of the cuffs, featured in black fishnet, tied up with black satin ropes, and secured at both ends by French bowline knots. She had gotten his warped wit from day one, on occasion granting him an outright guffaw. His college roommate was furious with her. "Don't laugh! It only encourages him!" In fact, it was an early clue that she was The One. Other persuasive evidence was laid bare in the frantic months of clutch and cling before he was off to war, those two long years ago.

Through eyelids drooped by sapped libido, he sagged back on the love-soaked pallet to soak up Miss Afterglow's ample assurance—and the further promise of weekend's first light—that there was plenty more to be had where this came from ... to feast his eyes on the busy morning's surfeit of honey, drizzling from hot biscuit into warm ladle for a tasty lapping up ... to muse in wonderment that he, the epitome of Mr. Terrified-To-Commit, was actually here, absorbing this nuptial countdown without a drop of panic. At least not yet.

In other words, to reflect on how he came to be this sopping, lapping lucky.

He confessed to himself that the interminable last two years had been the clincher. Absence does make the heart pound faster, doubtless an evolutionary ploy to get some iota of a man's blood to his brain. By night he would lay awake conjuring her into his arms. By day she cavorted among his thoughts like an implacable sylph. Even her few actual visits passed as if fleeting make-believe, flying to his embrace for a non-stop blur of draining ecstasy, only to vanish back into thin air. Still Mr. Terrified had hesitated. The more he wanted her to always be there, the harder it became to tell her so—a paradox owed to the ghost from his past.

ONCE UPON a lifetime ago he had pledged himself to another—a claim staked on impulse by a boy buoyed by lofty stakes. Not to suggest that the impetuous pledge had proved thankless. His wasn't a selfless *c'est la vie*, some noble but lost knight in tarnished armor flinging himself onto a dull and rusty sword. She was a fine catch and they were an obvious couple. Ask anyone. Yet as the day loomed close when he must seal their eternity, he had grown increasingly torn. On a sunny June afternoon he'd interrupted the final arrangements for their conjugal sarcophagus—the gleeful bride-to-be gushing over scrolled silverware patterns and embossed ceremonial napkins—to say he couldn't do it. Each place setting cost as much as an engine rebuild, while the stark metallic script and ornate silver bells fanned out before him on ruffly white squares proclaimed a date just three weeks away! Christ, when did all this happen? The icy pit in his stomach (honed and polished sword tip?) had told him they would both regret it. Maybe now, maybe later. Hell, maybe not for their entire interment. How was he to know?

Haunted by his betrayal, he had vowed to his countermanded conscience, "Never, ever, again."

And why would he? What free male wouldn't avoid that dread Day Of No Return? "They'll do anything for their M-R-S Degree," wagged the tongues of buddies and strangers, "then see what they'll do." "Don't get TIED DOWN," clamored macho monthlies and the silver screen, "It's the old 'Gotta' trap. First 'You gotta change this' then 'You gotta change that.'"

The prophecy for a bachelor's nuts in a nutshell: capitulation, subjugation, oppression. Buried alive, and too emasculated to ring the rescue bell.

But without warning, whether on a ribald wager or voyueristic whim, the gods had bestowed Angela to ring his bells. Angela, the breathtaking embodiment of everything he dare not believe might—after all—exist. Angela, who brightened everything in his universe. Who knew of his ghost, but braved herself anyway. Who, when she could possess any man she desired, seemed to actually desire him.

How could she possibly be other than a wishful illusion?

Well, she might be make-believe, but she made a hot-blooded male wonder: must the hunt always end with the catch? More to the point, must the catch always end with the hunt?

Either way, there would be no catch and release this time. Granted, a catch as scrumptious as this lip-smacker was most likely the wishful illusion she seemed—a fantastic figment of his deprived imagination, a *pièce de non-résistance* wrought by ignited passion. But, man alive, making out with her sure made a guy want to make off with her. So let the Playboy Philosophy go shaft itself. He had never gotten past the air-brushed glossies to read it anyhow. His motto would be,

Nothing hunted, nothing caught,
May our honeymoon ne'er be for naught.

Or, in the spirit of "more to the point,"

Here comes the groom—Fire in the hole!

Thus it came to pass that he, Mr. Terrified, had finally faced up to life's ultimate leap of faith … and where more fitting to petition a jumping partner than the precipice of Lover's Leap? He had whisked her off to its invigorating overlook on a magical December eve—a deep winter's faerie faerie night that turned breath to faerie frost and snow to faerie sparkles. The faeries tittered underfoot, transforming grumpy crunches into squeaks of delight. He threw himself to one knee, heart pumping. Toes numb. The waterfall frozen. Considered frostbite, got back up. Huge flakes swirled about her rosy cheeks like an enchanting snow globe, a magic moment to cradle forever. And inspiration for what to try next. Summoning the staunch resolve of a Hollywood leading man, he framed her quizzical upraised face between mammoth goose down survival mittens. He realized this time he'd better ask quick. And loudly.

"Yes, doofus," had come her quick and loud reply from between pinned ears, "I wouldn't want life to be boring."

As if. While the honeymoon menu remained to be seen—a gnawing unease he kept to himself—for now he knew he could come on in her kitchen anytime to hot biscuit with honey all a-drizzle. And on this long-awaited weekend he had arrived with an extra swagger in his step. Well, he thought, puffing up: given what he had wangled over the last couple years, capped by last night's harrowing ordeal, hadn't he earned it?

W HEN THE Air Force called him up from ROTC, they had plenty of distant spots to send a lovelorn lieutenant with a Master's in electronic communications. He'd been miserable. Forget Heartbreak Hotel. He found an even cheaper place to dwell, down at Motel Masochism. He wallowed in one pitiful self-pity pit after another, seeking perverse solace in songs of lovers stabbed through the heart—usually by way of the back. He played them far into the night on his old Martin guitar, cracking a bit more with each tune. After his first long trip he collected his per diem … and nearly fell over. Great Golden Goose—twenty-five dollars a day! Easily three times what he spent on those holes. Another year of this, and—yes!—his pity cash fund could make their fanciful wish come true.

And so Motel Masochism became Jackpot Junction. The savings multiplied until he could wait no longer to spring his surprise. Last night he'd driven hell bent for biscuit from his base in Illinois.

Would he ever learn?

The instant the radar trap had blipped on his Town and Country radio he'd known he was screwed—and in none of the ways his mind had been contemplating. What followed was like a nightmare in quicksand: The surreal home basement courtroom. The ill-tempered judge with his rumpled sleeping robe and watery, bloodshot eyes. The ultimatum, gaveled down with a leer. "This here's Southern I-ow-aaa, boy, and you just done broke the law. You wanna see that little gal a-yores tonight, you plead guilty to me and mah faithful gun-totin' deputy, right here and now. Then pay whatever I say and you'll be back on yore high-tailin', young buck way."

Now, sprawled on the sodden pallet, he savored his "deerly"-purchased freedom and the lingering aroma of a hardy "Lover Award" breakfast—an impromptu award blatantly cooked up to hasten his return to hardiness. He regarded the humble apartment of his long-order cook with the sort of fond memories that flood a young buck. Like the first time he brought her home. Whrooof! She was—

"Hello in there." Angela's voice and snapping fingers returned him from the thrilling days of yesteryear—to the one he had planned for today.

"Huh? Oh, sorry. Just remembering when a doe-eyed Dream Girl first paralyzed me in her headlights."

"Humph. Always sweetening up something with that tongue of yours, aren't you?"

"Hey, just call 'High-Low Silver' and your Lone Danger will be there."

"I'm sure. Speaking of silver tongue, did mining my tonsils convince you I'd like to open the other present?"

THE APARTMENT BUILDING shook from a thunderous domino of railcars in the switchyard outside—a reminder of his early efforts to get coupled up with her. He had offered a ride home the night they met in their off-campus guitar class. Nix. The second night. Nix. Miss Becoming was becoming a bummer. Class note: must be why they call it the blues. He assumed it was a "big brother" brush-off. She had acted scandalized when it spilled that he was five years older than her nubile nineteen. But he couldn't keep his eyes off her and kept dropping hints. "Brrrr, they say it's certain frostbite tonight and, oh boy, look—your legs are almost entirely exposed" … "Wherever those legs are taking you, I'm taking that direction too" … "I hear there's a pack of rabid leg-chomping dogs loose between here and—Where did you say you live?"

Months later, after much prodding and with a flaming blush, she had recounted her own thoughts at the time. For openers, she didn't know any other guy who drove, so assumed he was merely being polite. Besides, she liked to walk, especially beneath the starry expanse of a crystalline winter's night. She would stare up and ponder the vast mysteries of the universe. Burning questions like, "What is the Sweet Mystery of Life? And will I ever find it?" Anyhow, it was a trifling mile to her apartment, the wind chill was seldom more than twenty or thirty below, and new snows buried most of the ice.

Still she found herself tempted by Mr. Ride's persistent offer, however unnecessary. Even when his Adonis hazel eyes summarily dispatched her clothes, undoing each and every button, zipper, snap, and clasp with disconcerting deftness. For some reason she had that effect on males. Heck, she could swear there were girls who stopped in their tracks, smitten. But this wasn't one of her puppy dog admirers. This was a man. A man whose insatiable gaze told her she had something Mr. Ride wanted. And by the measure of his manliness she had it in spades. She also suspected "it" entailed more than sightseeing, a notion that gave her an oddly-pleasant flush of longing—a feeling both warm and cold, full and empty at the same time.

So this is what "hot-to-trot" feels like! Her older sister had said she would know it when she felt it, though this felt more like hot-to-gallop. Much to her chagrin the telltale flush rose to her face and glowed there, thanks to Mr. Ride's amused hazel eyes and other distractions. For crying out loud, she might as well have been the neon Miss Weatherball, stuck on a prominence for all eyes to learn what's next.

When Miss Weatherball is glowing red, warmer weather's just ahead.

"Warmer than this? Goodness gracious!" sounded the alarm of Mother's Good Little Girl, self-righteous Victorian pest that she was. She surveyed the cause for concern, then adjusted the glasses on her buttoned-up nose to see if she was seeing what she thought she saw and not just seeing what she was thinking she thought she saw. "My, oh my!" she said, glasses rooted to what she saw actually was what she thought she saw and not just what she had thought she thought she saw. "Whatever have you in mind for *that*? Mercy me!"

"What is it with you, the birds, and the beeswax," grumped Miss Weatherball. She clipped their nails to make ready for some hot guitar licks. "You needn't get all a-fluster, tizzy-head. I'm only giving us a nice long peak to see what the fuss is about. Don't be such a ... a ... prissy prig!"

Week after deprived week Good Little Girl and her cute little axe drove him crazy. He had to have her. He discovered a plucky new charm that should have been stamped "CAUTION. FOR EMERGENCY USE ONLY." While maintaining a respectable hands-free zone, he hovered over her demure five-foot-four with his ramrod six feet of military bearing. Without a word, he would impose his imposing roddy-ness and glare down the other rutting classmates that tried to circle in on her, besotted by her bookish, babe-in-the-"woulds" innocence.

A bookish babe that remained innocent even as she rocked their black cat bones all night long, her scorching little axe working its mojo overtime.

By the close of week two he was a basket case. Was he to live out his years a chivalrous madman, forever pining for this pert little patootie, this moon-eyed music muffin with the Vargas Girl legs?

Fortunately, the third week was the charm that saved him. On that momentous evening he wooed Good Little Girl into her Victorian wool coat, escorted her to his carriage, and held open the passenger door—all the while thinking himself the rascal who would worm his way around the *tête-à-tête*, 'ere the parlor's dawn awakened his angel of the morning.

When she swung those sheer stockinged stunners of hers into his car, his every vital organ had leapt at the sight. With pointed elation and racing heart he dallied by the open door to pore over her divine form. Sweet Aphrodite, so this is how you find religion. As he inched the door shut on the love goddess vision, he mouthed a fervent prayer ... then reconsidered, aghast at his request. Where had this cad slithered from? This scumbag. This salty dog.

Well, to be fair, he was genuinely deprived. Were there sympathy for that devil he could make a kind-hearted woman study evil all the time and a young girl weep to be his savior. But never mind his hardship. For this young girl he should fall to his knees in the slush of the gutter and substitute a request worthy of her virtue.

Too late—his dual exhaust was doing him in. He could but hope for the best. He weaved around to the driver side and ventured in beside her. More woozy-headedness, plus his innards swooping into a Welkonian waltz. What bizarre affliction was this? Fighting for equilibrium, he turned to her, nose-to-nose in the old Ford's confines ... and sealed his fate. He wheeled above the clouds, a total goner on Love Potion Number One.

Plainly the gods were in cahoots, because on arrival Good Little Girl had whirled and squeaked, "Would you like to come in?" Whereupon her hands flew to her crimson face in a silent scream of horror, as if the forward suggestion had emanated from an alien body-snatcher. But forwardness is Cupid's pointiest arrow, and so, without further mortification, they had cozied right here on these same rust orange floor pillows, this same avocado green carpet, with these same Martin guitars. "What songs do you know? 'Four Strong Winds'? Hey, me too. What key? G? I play it in C. No problem, I'll capo at the seventh fret." Yeah, this duet definitely had potential. The evening flew. Her roommate—zikes, her older sister, this could be tricky—kept breezing by to check on them. Song after melancholy song, their mood poured out. "Where Have All the Flowers Gone," "The Cruel War," "Until It's Time for You to Go." Damn, what was this? And then—

"KNOCK, KNOCK, anyone home?" Angela was rapping on his head.

"Huh? Tonsils. Yes. Tonsils like that get you anything you want." With a sonorous "Ta Da!" to cover for his clambering heart, he produced the colorful package from behind his back. She took it and waved it before his eyes. "Very funny. Yes, I'm still here," he said.

"Well, try to stay awhile. This has me really curious." She shook the present. "A smidge heavier, eh? Don't tell me. This must be the matching Junior LaRue lashy thingy." She bounced up and down. "Goody! Goody!"

"All right, already, Miss Marquise de Sarcasm. Just open it."

She tore into the little green box with its bright red ribbon and big silver bow. Flipped through its contents. Looked up—baffled. "*Europe on Five Dollars a Day*? What's this for?"

"Uh … check the three bookmarks."

"Okaaay. London, check. Paris, check. Rome … Umm, wait a minute. You don't by any chance mean—"

"I do mean. As in 'Leaving on a Jet Plane,' except we both get it on, er, get on it." He knew he sounded like an LP on a runaway Victrola, but he couldn't crank the words out fast enough. "And—you absolutely won't believe this—you've got a whole month and eight days to prep and pack! How's that for notice? Not that you'll need a lot of clothes, mind you. Come to think of it, what you're wearing can be your trousseau! You know, as in 'We see London, we see France, who needs Angie's underpants?'"

She currently had on, from top to bottom, his long flannel shirt and—nothing. Bare legs extended from shirttails in a piece-offer "V." Make love not war, they entreated. Ah, the bitter irony: to prove worthy of such a piece a man must march off to war. Until his return to embrace her evermore, let the "V" be for vanquish. He was hers to surmount as pleased her.

In fact, her toes had already made headway at his jeans zipper ... but stopped when she heard his news. She sat speechless, no doubt amazed at his tenacious grasp of every essential. To further that amazement, he slinked his hand through the carpet and tenaciously grasped her foot. Then, employing the practiced stealth of a master, proceeded up her ankle.

"Just think, kiddo. Our first three full-time weeks together! Ever! The undress rehearsal of what to do 'til death do us part. The inaugural ball for our fairytale romance."

"But ... but ... ball our way across Europe?" she sputtered, "In five weeks? With my final exams and graduation in three weeks? Have you gone off the deep end and bashed your head on a jutting rock?"

Excellent. Her deep exam of where they were headed had graduated her to be gone off on their big bash. And for you, darling, I will jut from my rocks to the very final end. Indeed, I sense that you already know this.

He pressed on, gesticulating with his free hand to sum up and punctuate the salient details. "Yes, Angie. Three weeks, around the clock, to do whatever we want. Think about it. It's sure all I can think about." He advanced his stealth hand up her leg.

"Trust me, your line of thought is palpable, but ..." She faltered. Trailed off. Straightened up and resumed, "... but international travel must be terribly expensive. Since when is an Air Force Lieutenant so loaded?"

She was hooked and reeled in. Now to land her. "I'm glad you're sitting, because say hello to the new Mr. Responsible. It's all paid for! Well, um, the airfare anyway." He stifled a nervous cough and hurried on. "Special military charter, New York to London. Coach." He stressed the last word and imagined waving a star-trailing wand as his glittering, glass-slippered bride ascended a flower-strewn staircase to her regal perch. He would have busted his buttons if he'd been wearing his shirt—which turned his thoughts to the bust that was busting its buttons now. He started his hand up under the flannel.

"My, my, Mister—*ahem*—Responsible, I'm truly impressed, but—Hey! How did you get up here?" She pulled his arm and the shirt back down. "Let me concentrate, you one-track wonder. Now, where were you? I mean, where am I? Wait, no, who am I?—was I? Phooey!" She shut her eyes tight, pressed her fingers to her temples, and spoke in slow, measured words. "Let's see. So we fly out of New York City? And I suppose Ferdie has to get us there?"

Why did she sound so skeptical? Time for more cunning. He stretched out his long legs and leaned back to play up an auspicious likeness to the Eiffel Tower—that other honeymoon destination erected foremost for fun, but giving rise to every outcome conceivable. "And why wouldn't Ferdie get us there?" he replied, affecting the air of nary a care. "I'll treat him to all new points and plugs. Check his fluids. Make sure his rubber doesn't leak."

She groaned. "So begins the honeymoon humor. And, yes, I catch the drift. My big bad wolf won't have to grapple with those little dread riding hoods much longer."

"Grrrr, that would make it worth my turning twenty-seven," he said. The Pill, that holy grail of free willfulness. He could hardly contain himself until then.

She craned her neck and bulged her eyes to scan his Eiffel-ness—a tad theatrical in his humble opinion, though he should have foreseen his elevated appeal. "My heavens, Lieutenant!" she said, her close inspection concluded. "Clearly that mission has your full attention. I suppose it's the real reason you want to get married on your birthday. And here I assumed it's so you'll never forget our anniversary."

"Well, truth be known, I hope for both," he admitted. How did she do that?

"Are all communication engineers so hot-wired and spacey?"

"How do you think Sputnik got up there? We like to put electrifying young things into orbit."

She patted his optimal entry trajectory. "Still proud of yourself, aren't you?" Her eyebrows shot up. "Holy Hot Spot, Missile Man! Has launch sequence initiated? Maybe we ..."

As she fussed over him, he recalled when he first took her out. He wasn't built for subtlety. Even Miss Innocence had figured out where his heads-up was headed with her go-ahead. Luckily she was a dedicated science major, raring to learn animal practices in the wild. Meanwhile she had heeded her wise sister's observant tip—"Don't advertise your man"—and gotten him to switch from light cotton pants to dark blue jeans "for less conspicuous happiness." He couldn't help that she rendered him Mr. Virility Showpiece. All he had to do was eye her, hear her voice, touch her, or—God help him—smell her, for his epic exuberance to attract the notice of every female in sight.

"... but before I light your booster," she was saying, "what's the date our plane leaves New York?"

Whew, one more question, then ignite me, hothips. He opened his mouth to answer ... but no words came out.

"Oh-oh. What's with the oval lips, Missile Man?"

"I'm sure the date's nothing to worry about. Let's play a tune." He dove for his guitar and busied himself with the large, resounding Dreadnought in a cacophony of accessorizing and tuning.

"The date. Now. This New Yorker insists." she said, tapping her petite instrument with her fingerpicks.

H ER ADORABLE little Martin—inimitable reminder of what almost never happened. It was his final year of grad school, no time for frivolity. Yet something had drawn him to jump-start 1969 with that one last blues guitar class. He had found the quirky building, paused at the door, decided to go on in, and ... froze. He tried his officer-and-gentle-man best not to ogle, but failed. Dismally. He degenerated into a seedy seed-bearing ogler, like all the other strutting males in the room. Referring, of course, to every student but her. She sat in the front row, oblivious, Guitar God's gift to picky men—short dress, heart-stopping legs, golden brown hair down to there, jagged green bottleneck on left pinky—tuning her fittingly-pristine, small-body o-16NY. A girl to make music with? A girl that made you pinch yourself and hope you didn't wake up? Inconceivable. She would have to be straight from heaven. "Hi, what's your name?" he had heard himself ask. She blushed. Looked down. Fluttered her lashes. "Angela," came her mellifluous reply.

Sweet Angie, slide guitar angel, emerald green winter jumper clinging like soft felt to sublime sophomore curves. He might as well have proposed on the spot.

"Well?" she said, tapping louder and flashing a bolt out of the blue eyes that could make him do anything.

Criminy, what if he had turned from that door? What if she hadn't finally accepted that ride home? What if she had gone for the rich dandy with the D'Angelico? What if—

"Am I delirious, or are you actually marrying me?" he said.

"When aren't you delirious? As for marriage, that may depend on when the plane leaves," she said, her frostbite tone evoking Lover's Leap—as a solo descent.

"December twentieth?" he chirped.

"The twentieth! Did your one-track mind derail in the Tunnel of Lust? We get married on the eighteenth! When we'll have been apart another bleak, wretched, empty five weeks! And you know doggone well you've got me crazed already, going on and on about a bouncy king-size hotel bed. The one thing you've let slip about our mystery bridal suite, when—Aha! I knew it! That smug twitch just now tells me there's even more up your sleeve, isn't there? Or should I say up your pants? And what does *that* suggest about our chances of a sensible, rational, realistic road start nice and early on the nineteenth?" She stopped for breath and tossed up her hands.

An entrancing image bounced before him, faster and faster, keeping time with some insistent beat. He shook himself and found her tapping up a storm. "I'm sorry," he said, "Can you repeat everything after 'bed'?"

"Get that goofy grin off your face and focus! How long does it take to drive from Minneapolis to New York?"

"Don't worry, how could Ferdie not make it by the Twentieth?" he said, and launched into a take on their warmup song. "It ain't no use to stew and ponder why, babe," he sang with gusto and a flurry of riffs on his D-18.

Angela sighed, ripped into the bass run of "Key to the Highway," and belted out, "Ferdie's gonna roam this highway, until the day we die ..."

PART II: THE *COUPÉ*

SO HERE THEY WERE in the middle of the night, Ferdie crawling along the Pennsylvania Turnpike in fog worthy of a Led Zeppelin concert. Daniel strained over the steering wheel to follow the shoulder of the road, it's ghostly white line clueing him onward in a soporific stupor. Mile. By. Dazed and Confused. Mile.

He knew that off in the blackness to the side awaited a rollover ditch and desolation row of one frozen field after another. He really ought to install a couple of those stupid retrofit seatbelts. Rats. No more stealing a feel in your automobile, your baby beside you at the wheel? He heaved a sigh. What would it take to top your hotrod, an arm around your girl, free to come together on a nice long ride?

He heard a faint grumbling and peered over at Angela. The grumble segued into a soft whistle, and she reached up to trace a finger across the lofty interior of the aging Ford. He hadn't realized she was that taken with Ferdie's Crown Victoria funkiness. The extra headroom had gone out of style with the "long, low" look of '57, but was bound to come in handy somehow.

She stopped and turned to him, appearing surprised to find him on the honeymoon. "So, how are Ferdie and my space cadet husband doing?"

Strange. Was that a slight edge in her voice?

"Ferdie is real bored. He's built for speed, not schlepping down an empty expressway at twenty miles per hour."

"Real bored. Aren't you punny tonight."

She was so quick. He'd always been attracted to smart girls, but Miss Encyclopedia was one for the whole case of books. She and he could talk about anything. And talk. And talk. She'd even listened to how he had souped up his beloved '56 Crown Vic: Its bored-and-stroked 312 cubic inch Thunderbird engine with dual exhaust and ECZ high compression heads, fueled by "The Holley Trinity"—the three oversize double-barrel carburetors he hand-filed to cram onto an Edelbrock intake manifold instead of the usual Stromberg 97s. Its custom dual points, multi-gap plugs, balanced crankshaft, and chrome tachometer. Its overdrive transmission with the Hurst floor play he strong-armed in to replace the oinker stock slush box. Plus the bat-out-of-hell swapped rear end—a rare police interceptor differential, scrounged in a back alley with the crane truck from his dad's machine shop. Then there was—

The car convulsed in Ferdie's depths—the jolting rattle of something big wanting out of its cage.

Damn. The drive shaft again. Damn. Damn. *Et tu, Brute?* Well, he knew better than to gloat about his car on a road trip. And Mr. Preventive Maintenance knew he should've replaced the U-joints. But, noooo, Mr. Procrastinator was certain they'd last the trip. After all, they were only the most pummeled victims of his lead Bullitt foot. Only what connects the engine to the rear wheels. Only what keeps the drive shaft from tearing free and catapulting the car end over end. He bonked himself upside the head. What had he gotten them into now? Bonk. If it's not one thing it's another. Bonk. Bonk.

It worked. Like a lightbulb jiggled in a loose socket, his head buzzed and fizzed with bright ideas. He eased up on the gas and the car's vibration went away. "Yep, Ferdie," he announced, "Resonance. Varying the speed a mite ought to hold us together. More or less. At least until New York, eh old boy?"

Next on the list, rethink bachelor habit of talking to car out loud.

"We're not going to make it are we?" Angela sounded somewhat alarmed, but whether at his bond with an object of dubious merit or at the prospect of their demise *à trois* he decided not to ask.

"Fear not, Mrs. Raring-to-Go. Your Mr. Glad-to-Oblige has it all figured out. A while ago one of those honker eighteen-wheelers raced by like we were standing still. Their drivers are up so high they probably see above this blanket, right? Leastways, they sure drive like they do. So the next time one shoots past, I simply try to catch up and stay with him. What could possibly go wrong?"

"Uh-huh. Tell me, my ever-ready obliger, does testosterone dictate all of your plans? Because I think you'd better wake me when it's over." She was soon zonked out, a scarlet tinge on her Cheshire face.

AS WELL there should be. Either he had spent last night with one ex-maiden exceedingly happy to be married, or with a harem of taxingly talented triplets—each bending over some unique way to outdo the others. Every contender had introduced her consummate performance as a preview of coming attractions, hissing into his ear three little words guaranteed to make a man smile:

"Enjoy the show."

First there was Annie the Acrobat on the trampoline bed. Her act should've had a safety net. Next he encountered Fanny the Fish in the mermaid-go-round whirlpool tub. How did they not drown? And to finish him off, when he thought he already was, there appeared the drool-inducing Mystery Girl in her daring disguise: three mint lick-offs and an emerald green mask. Who was that delicious dolloped doll on the free-wheeling dessert cart? The sundae sweetie was stacked like a movie star, her audition more moving than any escapade in "Candy." Well, whoever that revolving indulgence was, gimme s'more of her. Lights! Action! Roll 'em!

The lights grew to a glare in his rear view mirror. What the—? He snapped out of his consuming rerun as a semi trailer truck roared by with flashing high beams and a blast from its air horn. Angela stirred. Daniel mashed the accelerator to the floor. The progressive linkage yanked the three Holleys wide open and the overdrive switch under the floored gas pedal kicked the tranny down into third gear.

The engine coughed, fell deathly silent, Daniel's hands clammy on the cold scallop grip of the steering wheel. Then the custom ignition caught the flood of fuel, the hopped-up V-8 let out a tri-powered roar, the tach jumped, and the prowler rear end burned rubber.

None too soon. A short distance ahead the semi's entire panoply of red taillights and yellow running lights vanished. In the sudden, terror-filled void, Daniel lost track of both truck and shoulder. Time froze and his brain screened an impending-death rerun of his life. Just as it got to last night's carte blanche, he was distracted by an annoying glimmer in the murk. It could be anything—the truck, a street lamp, an oncoming vehicle. Jesus, it might be Saint Peter extending a fistful of halos. Whatever it was, he'd know in a balls-out moment. His grudging brain shelved the skinflick and he aimed for the light, Ferdie's V-8 screaming out a three-deuce chorus of Holley-lujahs.

The truck materialized at his hood ornament. Daniel hit the brakes. Again the lights faded in the mist. He returned to the throttle in a hunt for the sweet spot. He'd have to kiss the truck's ass from here on in. If he slowed and lost sight he'd fly off the road with no sense of direction. The anonymous transport was his lone beacon in an unforgiving cloud, though for all he knew he was following Lucifer straight to the gates of Hell. He dropped back into overdrive and settled to the task. It promised to be a long and unnerving night, but their only chance of making New York in time.

"We'll chase this lunatic as far as we can," he said. Angela's head lolled to one side, lip magnets chafed and puffy. Better get Miss Kissy-face another crate of Chapstick. Her groggy mumbles lapsed back into a smooch-smacking dream—X-rated, judging by that familiar pussy smirk on her Angela-in-Wonderland mouth. Sheesh, if she could sleep through that ...

But she had never driven a car. She acted heedless of what thirty-three hundred pounds of twisted steel can do. You'd think she was tootling along on amusement ride tracks in Lollipop Land, the only care in her world being what new flavor to try next. He recalled some of his solo spinouts and close calls—those would have changed her perspective in a hurry. Doing 110 miles per hour across half of Minnesota to his roommate's wedding. Hitting 145 near red-line on a dark rural night, a sheared-off headlight rim shattering the windshield. Going airborne over a rise in a downtown drag race, trunk flying open on touchdown at an unexpected stop light.

Talk of testosterone. Well, he would have better use for it now. So many missed nights and days to make up for. At least they would catch up in style. Up. Up. All he could think about was her. He Eiffeled against the steering wheel. Too bad he had to keep driving. Man, he was so revved he could cycle in four strokes himself.

But how does she feel? Maybe it'll be different for her now. They seemed to have it all. But had it been too good to be true? Was she too good to be true? Granted, no icy pit this time. And his only musings on a sword quite pointedly pleasant. Like last night. Say, who was that masked merrymaker anyway? And would she ever reappear?

But the bridal suite was behind them now, wasn't it? It brought to mind the time he had to console his former roommate, a few months after the poor wretch tied his ill-fated noose. The sad story unfolded over schooners of tear-salted beer: How the father-in-law fixed a bell to the connubial bed. How on the first night the tawdry tipster had pealed 'til dawn. Yet how since then it seemed but apathy for whom the bell tolled.

What had most alarmed Daniel about this revelation was that his ex-roomy was one of those legendary scalawags you couldn't help but like. The one you wanted on your side, like the time he shattered Ferdie's plastic dome light cover doing Lord knows what … only to return from his next all-night bender with the back seat level full of pilfered replacements. The Madcap Maestro of Midnight Auto Supply, beaming his pearly whites. He partied and gambled and flashed his devil-sent dimples. He was the real deal, the wanted poster for the All-American Bad Boy. The irrepressible prick that the babes got in line for.

If Mr. Serial Stud was summarily spurned, what chance did All-American Doofus—Mr. Goofy Grin himself—have?

H E HEARD Angela clear her throat. He turned to find her stunningly revived, a dish dished up for hungry eyes—right arm along the passenger door, left arm on the seat back, *crème de la crème* legs among a saucy presentation of appetizers. Arrrooo, she was one scrumptious *soufflé*. Loaded, part of him couldn't help thinking, with fresh eggs. Ferdie's complicit heater fan supplied gourmet peeks under her waffling cotton dress. The trifling pink tease was his summer favorite, and she'd surprised him by bringing it on the trip despite the season. Its simple daisy print suggested Haight-Ashbury, her springy curls the flowers in her hair. Dash lights and reflection off the fog suffused with the plucked-blossom glow of his flower child bride. Her only assent to winter: long, fuzzy stockings. Emerald green.

He fought to focus back on the car. Have gun but must travel. He hummed a ditty about keeping his mind, hands, and snoopy eyes on anything except that naughty little scamp of a dress scampering from her calendar girl figure. And those damn stockings, their giddy-up green directing him to her go go girl intersection like a pair of don't-stop signals—with Mr. Eiffel at the wheel.

"I miss you tonight," Daniel said, in a puberty-like yodel.

"Uhhh, it's rather hard to not notice." She batted her lashes at him. "And I notice it's almost to where it can honk for me. Hurry it up, will you? I'm horny myself just watching it get there."

Good grief. Would he get used to this? "You're unbelievable," he said.

She laughed. "Speak for yourself, Tarzan."

"OK. You Jane. Tarzan need. Keep up all night."

"Hmmm, really?"

Oops. Foolhardy choice of words. What has Tarzan started this time?

She rubbed her left foot along his thigh and propped her right heel on the padded dash. The scurrilous dress scurried back, baring her raised leg from bootwear to booty. "Did you know Jane still wet from last night?" she said. An impish twinkle in her eye and shift of her legs invited him to check for himself.

Ho, boy. Swinging from vines would be less hazardous than this.

He ran his hand along her goose bumps to aid and abet the high-tailing dress. Up her thigh. Over her hip. To her waist! He broke into a sweat. Was anything more deliberate, not to mention cocksure, than a girl in your car sans underpants?

Well, mayhaps when she sported that skimpy lace come-and-get-it for her First Time. ("Don't be so dumbstruck," she had announced. "Yes, it's emerald green. Let's get going, teacher-man. As you've so often sized up and pointed out to me, I've put you off far too long!") Talk about devotion to lessons. By day three Miss Gung-Ho Student had dubbed the fetching little peek-a-boo her "trusty Irish school flag" because—no matter when, where, or how she flourished it—one glimpse of what he called "that wee juicy thing" always brought her Danny Boy on the run.

Harking back to her earliest one-on-one he delved deep, greeted by a quaver. "Mmm, there you are," she whispered. She laid back and closed her eyes.

Last night's production couldn't be missed. He brought it onto center stage and conducted an encore. She shuddered. She clapped her hands over his. The finale played out between his fingers. She smiled.

Jane so easy.

"My turn," she said, pulling herself together. She bent down to work at his buckle.

She knew how to keep him awake alright. "You're teeming with surprises tonight," he managed to say.

"All your doing, Tarzan-the-Prolific. Let's see what else that un-hooded big bad wonder has in store, shall we?"

HE STRUGGLED to concentrate on the truck lights while she lowered his zipper, groped, sprung his prolific, un-hooded, big bad wonder free. She growled an ardent, "Well, well, hello there, my Tarzanic Treat, you Gorgeous Gift to Girl-world, you," and fell on him with tigress tongue, cobra fingers, entwining tresses. His temples drummed to her jungle rhythm. He felt as much as heard the feral rumbles in her throat. Her gusto reminded him up and down of last Saint Patrick's Day, how thoroughly her emerald green lipstick had—

She stopped and peered up. Uh-oh. He'd learned to spot that double-dare-you gleam day or night, wherever they might be, regardless of weather. Same difference, her clothes cast off for ventilation or cast off to get warmed up.

What chancy undertaking was next on her agenda?

Her face flushed and eyes blazing, she latched onto him with Red Baroness clutches—one at the base, the other higher up—and popped a matrimonial question not to be refused. "Would you like ... to revisit last night ... using this?" She strained at her cumbrous joystick hold, but seemed not to mind when the joystick grew even more cumbrous. "Can you ... move the seat ... back a little?" she asked, battling for breath as well as grip.

Great guns, here we go again. Make way to maneuver behind that action-happy tail of hers. Only, this time—

in the front seat

while driving

blind.

Now he couldn't breathe either. At this rate they'd both pass out. Well, shoot, what better way to go? Here's to low oxygen, ample cockpit, and long arms. He rammed away from the steering wheel. "Make yourself comfortable," he said, ample cockpit at the ready, one long arm going for her dress.

She slapped his hand. "Unh-unh-unh," she chided, "a few questions first." She sat up, schoolmarm straight, and fiddled at the diminutive dress as if to contrive it into a prim and proper concealment. Then, in a cheery lilt, "What say we begin with, 'On which date did you first try to unzip my jeans?'"

He gaped at her, numbed by this abrupt and convoluted treason. "You mutinous urchin!" was all he could ejaculate, "You can't mean to play this game now!"

"Silly. Do you want my clothes off or not? There's not so many, I promise. And surely you're not still in a snit over that layered ensemble I suckered you with like last time?" She tickled him under the chin and added, in her most irksome cootchy-coo voice, "You poor baby."

"Stop that! It chills me all over!"

"Goodness, aren't you the sensitive one. We'd best get on with my little quiz, don't you think?" She plied his right ear with ardor-slickened lips and his left with a handful of long silky hair. "Hmmmm, lover boy?" she mouthed wetly, fingerstrolling into his orchard to squeeze some lemons and shake the peach tree.

The car juddered, passenger side tires blundering onto loose gravel. Pebbles *rat-a-tat-tatted* the undercarriage, like a trigger-happy troll capitalizing on a Chicago Typewriter to spell "TroubleTroubleTrouble." Daniel snatched the wheel with both hands to ease from the murderous shoulder back to his post between the rocks and a hard place, dead center on the truck's bumper.

Uff da! So the little vixen was out to play dirty, was she? He hunkered down and gave her a once-over to judge his odds. The two stockings and dress for starters, but who knew how many underthings? Her torture could go on and on. Ah, but wait, no panties. Perchance implying a shortcut? Yeah, that would work. In fact, the more he considered it—

As for her glasses, she was more than welcome to leave them on. Sure, "glasses off" was terrific, all erudition banished to the bedside stand. Legs in charge, no need for *Brittanica*. But then came the day she dragged in a mirror discarded by the unwitting neighbors next door to Daniel's bedroom. She had hustled to show the showtime value of "glasses on," reflecting an encyclopedic command of visionary leg experiments—with results measured in decibels. So now, given the car's interior rear view mirror and no wakened neighbors to pound on the wall—

"Uh, why not just come as you are?" he suggested suggestively.

Alas, the vixen was not out to play with dirty words. "Listen," she hissy fitted, "This first one is a giveaway and you know it. Are you going to answer the question, or do I dress for that snow out there?"

"Oh, excuuuse me, Miss Missing Knickers. You needn't get so hot under the … well, whatever you've got left to get hot under. The answer is—and, yes, I'm aware how shocked you were—it was our second date, which was February the Fourteenth. And shouldn't that count as two answers?" ·

"Nice try." She hooked her toes in the top of an emerald green stocking. Peeled it down her leg. Over her foot. Dangled it. Twirled it. Lobbed it into a corner.

A stirring reminder of other tricks her toes could do.

"Next question. What did I bring you and how did you react?"

"As though you'll ever let me forget. You showed up with a yummy pink cupcake topped with sticky cream frosting and red candy kisses. Then you had the nerve to accuse *me* of being forward, as if some magic Calendar Calendar On The Wall—Miss February perhaps?—should've alerted me that it was Valentine's Day, not some sugar-babe come-on. That you really were a wide-eyed innocent, sashaying hither and yon, mostly hither, your sweet behind so roundly conveying, 'Be mine, Candy Man!' And its waaaay-too-convenient zipper, smack rear center down over that teeny-bopper tush—a combo clearly concocted for couch quickies. Still, just a couple teeny cracks at it and I called it quits, you'll grant me that. Told you I needed a cold shower, and—Hey! Those were *two* questions, you callous, calculating, little conniver!" His indignant huff gusted into a snort.

"Tsk, tsk. Even more impatient than usual." She hummed "Summertime" and toiled at the other stocking. Rolled it down her shapely, lissome leg. Her graceful, high-arched foot. Her—

He slapped himself to refocus on the truck. "You cruel hold-out! Next question! And be quick about it!"

"Hrumph," she said, parading a hurt pout. "If you're going to snap at me and call me names, you deserve a riddle. How come—even when you blindfold me and stuff old Gabby with buckaroo choices—whatever I pick next always becomes my new ride 'em cowboy favorite … and yet my favorite has never changed?"

She reached to pull a stocking back on, awash in smug superiority—but he answered without hesitation. "Because your favorite is always whatever one we're trying."

Her jaw dropped. "How did you know that?" A withering glare accused him of having tallied secret score cards since Flag Day One.

He rolled his eyes. "Let's see, where do I begin? Possibly because every pick makes you yell, 'Whee, let's do that one from now on!'? Or because you whine and sulk every time we empty the hat? Then dash for your blindfold the minute we've rustled up the next hatful? Maybe because more and more you stay blindfolded even after you hand me your pick, insisting I surprise you with what it is—the, er, long and hard way? Or, as you like to put it, 'By crook and hook'? Other clues come to mind, Little Miss Gotta-Have-It-Bareback, but times a-wastin'. Keep unsaddling."

"Oh, so now you've added mind reader to the, um, various things you can do for me. Well, you just wait and see, you … you … rodeo boy!" she blustered. "You're in for a surprise or two yourself!"

STILL GROUSING under her breath—his ears perked up at "never seems to need stirrups" and "try this mustang, buster"—she grabbed her hem and started to slink off the dress, snaking it with sizzling slowness up her pearly bare skin. Each time he stole a ravenous glance she bubbled in unrepentant delight at his torment. His mouth went dry as she tarried, curve-by-taunting-curve, until her midriff joined in an eye-popping hula girl aloha. Hip hip hooray for no grass skirt. Which brought to mind how those hips had learned to express her hoorays. How that waist could hula its way through hatful after hatful. How that twisting tummy always shivered under his silver tongue.

Now for the coconuts.

She paused. He groaned. Mischief was written all over her. She flashed up the dress. He swiveled. Too late. He riveted to her next hike—and further vexation. "Golly, now it's stuck under this one," she chirruped, like some Rockette wannabe fresh off a train from Omaha. "Gee, caught on this one too. Gosh, how will I ever get it off over these?" She hoisted the left side. Joggle. The right. Joggle. Her face pinched with worry. Joggle, joggle.

The pitiless hussy had him shaking from the dank of his own musk, its randy fragrance betraying him at every pungent pore. Her shrewd eyes flicked over him and she appeared to marshal herself for one last Aphroditean effort. Had she whiffed his desperation? She hauled at the bodice, the meager fabric straining beneath its formidable contents. He watched from his miserable station behind the wheel with all the optimism of a libidinous kamikaze aiming an unstable craft in blind weather. This vaguely-disquieting metaphor he put out of mind when the fabric gave way and scuttled upward. His heart hammered. The hem snagged one rigid vanguard. The other. Teetered there. Was she out to explode his eyeballs? And the family jewels? Surely one itty-bitty tug …

Nope. A petulant lower lip decreed the task utterly futile. "Aw, shucks," she said, and released the laden hammock into a jostling jounce—exaggerated by a colossal sigh and shrug that fanned his smoldering suspicion into outright cynicism. Meanwhile the family jewels were hurting, and not just euphemistically.

Joggle, joggle. Giggle, giggle.

A Neanderthal noise rumbled in his throat. He furrowed his brow, bared his teeth, and turned … to a gleeful shriek and sailing pink blur. He blinked, stared, and nearly veered into the ditch again. Why, that scheming little—no bra either! She beamed a triumphant smile, arms flung up and fabulous ambrosial breasts bobbing free … flaunted like the *magnum opi* of an Off-Broadway showgirl … working him like a love-starved sailor on a one-night pass. He glimpsed her mouth-watering enticements, evocatively milk-white and full, through a lustrous curtain of honey brown hair. Peeking out here and there, the perky vessels swept up dangling clusters of speared curls and gamboled them about like exotic silk tassels. Lowering her hands, she laced her fingers behind her neck and blew him a warning kiss—then drew the coquette curtain high.

"How about it, hotshot," she wheedled, "Want to wait 'til New York for a piece of this cheesecake?"

Her delectable endowments swayed in all their bounteous glory, his blood pulsing stronger at each hypnotic high. From pendulum tips to plaything toes, she was devastating.

He wrenched his eyes back on the road, her Siren vision floating in his periphery. Was this a fantasy? Was he lost in a fatal reverie? He reached to find out. Exuding a visceral purr, Miss Moist New York Cheesecake daubed his fingertips and guided them up to her navel. He took the hint and kept going back for more, lavishing the love glaze over her magnificent nakedness like a blind *pâtissier* crowning a royal *vol-au-vent*. As he glossed each luscious morsel, he recalled its taste: Salt-stippled swale. Tangy mound. Permeating sweetness.

The purr grew distinctly audible.

"Geez, you are such a wet dream," he said in a husky croak. "I bet God Himself looks to you for His salivation."

"AND NOW to check you out, O Blasphemous One." She sidled her gooey tart across the vinyl upholstery and fancied it hot alongside him.

The car careened down the highway as she plundered his winterwear, oohing and aahing after each liberated layer. "Praise be!" she whooped, his final remnant airborne. "I'd say you can drive behind anything you want. All set to try two at once, you prodigious beast?"

Wasting no time for an answer, she jockeyed her left leg across his and swung astride his lap. She twisted the car's mirror to reflect a wink that boasted "Better rear view coming up" and skimmed her mate-bait mane over her shoulder in a cascade of long honey twirls—a tumble of temptation that declared,

> *Such perfection is for man to perpetuate,*
> *And man, oh man, are you the man for the job!*
> *But 'til your knock-up of this knockout just cannot wait,*
> *Why not practice all the ways man can knock?*

The comely, come-and-play tresses frolicked all down her bare back, skittering to a tee-hee-hee stop just above its dimpled contour—nature's handhold for in-depth results.

She presented the temptation-adorned handhold at a handy knock practice tilt.

Dear Munificent God Almighty, what that *bon appétit* eyeful of raised *derrière* did to him. He couldn't help it. She was his little French filly, prancing to be rounded up, any time, any place. A spirited young thing kicking the stable down to experience the enormous, vigorous, and copious appreciation of a victor who could measure up to her panoramic dreams.

Lordy, those thoughts she gave him. Should one circling leer at that cheeky prize always make him feel like such … well, such an animal?

The frisky little troublemaker was reading his mind again. She waggled at him, springy palomino tresses rolling atop her heavenly hillock like impudent, cartwheeling nymphs.

In hindsight, neither he nor she could keep a secret from the other for long. One salty afternoon in his den of iniquity, collapsed with her in spent disarray amongst a tangle of ravaged sheets, he had divulged his occasional, uh, equestrian twist. He'd hoped she would accept it as the tribute he intended. She had lowered her eyes and jabbed at his noisy mattress, its creaking, sproinging, and rasping the underlying accompaniment he counted on every time she got rambunctious—the mounting caterwaul of its overworked springs his secret to maintaining a cadence throughout her moans, outcries, and quasi-whinnies of approval … the neighbors' wall-pounding disapproval … and the bed's collapse. She hesitated at the freshest of the soggy areas she called their "overspills of joy" and, to his immense relief, squeegeed out a horseshoe-size smiley face. Having corralled her courage, she revealed her own shocking tribute. "Surely you can tell how I think of you whenever I wrangle you up behind me?" she said. She strayed a bold gaze over him and up to meet his astounded eyes. The rosy testimonial still dappled across her chest—a lingering chestnut mare red beneath her steamy summer tan—spread to her face with her torrid confession. "How can I help myself … when that's what you feel like to me?"

Invoking her five-legged tribute, he sprang for her—but she stopped to wag a finger at him instead. "Whoa there, my champing charger. Tut tut, aren't we pawing at the floorboards tonight? Before you pony up, Man o' War, I told you I had an extra surprise." She retrieved a clinking object from the glove box and snapped one end about her wrist. He couldn't believe it. Lash! She started the other end on her opposite wrist and raised her arms to the visor rod so he could see around her. Her eyebrows bobbled at him in the mirror and he heard a soft click that vowed, "To hold and to have. And have some more." She braced to her makeshift hitch rail.

He bolted to her, wild to perform the prodigious beast in her horseplay. Forcing his eyes back on Lucifer's twinkling transport, he steered the beckoning road with his left hand and her beckoning bottom with his right. Hurrying her with his thumb in the made-to-order small of her back, he lined her up and swung her legs wide astraddle with his knees. Giddy with anticipation, he prickled the instant she nudged on. But she held her stance and toyed with him there—dripping, dabbing, swirling—blending his own telling stickiness with hers into an *au naturel* topping. Off, on, and around she dripped and dabbed and swirled, murmuring to herself in a low, dreamy voice.

"Mmmmmmmm," intoned Dream Girl, licking her Dreamsicle lips.

THE TOPPING began to run, creeping down him in a warm spiral. Did she mean to drive him stark mad? The viscous warmth fingered out onto his tormented family jewels. He gritted his teeth and zeroed in on the lights flashing through the fog ahead, a pattern repeating brighter and brighter. That's when it hit him. Lucifer was trying to tell him something! Yes, ha-ha, so clear now, a message any fool could decode. It said, "T-A-K-E-!-H-E-R-!-Y-O-U-!-F-O-O-L-!"

He pushed like a man possessed, his breach swift, exhilarating—and superbly effortless. Angela arched back and sucked for breath with a startled "Eeep!" Then—facing the heavens in a rapturous trance, her exhale long and serene—she slid on down.

So desirous, so desirable, her trembling body seated Man o' War all the way and stiffened, ready. He ached to serve her right there … but resisted nature's all-fired rush. He would complete her in his own sweet time, determined to spread the fun of spreading her legs.

Honey moon-on-a-stick.

Tending to both truck and treat, he roamed his hand over her brandished torso. She flinched and shivered. He caressed her with her own soft hair, and she melted back against him. Scoopng around her waist and up, he hefted her overspilling bounty to cop a feel you'd never get in high school. The twin feasts prodded him for more as he nuzzled her neck and inhaled … *eau de menthe*. Mystery Girl! She was meant to be his! And to think he had ever hesitated. Talk about demented. How would he have ever again found anyone like her? Her enthusiasm, her adventurousness, her—

"You're mine! My wife!" he blurted.

She leaned forward and jolted him with a succulent squeeze. He marveled that her hands were still trussed to the visor. "I love the sound of those words," she said. She lifted. Lingered. Nibbled. Shocks rippled through him. "I love having you husband me!" She returned down his galvanized length. "I need you to do it now!" she whimpered. "I can't seem to stay off you!" She moved on him again. "I can't stay off!" And again. "I just can't!"

His reflex spoke for him (*On, girl, on! Stay, girl! Nice girl!*), and she started on and on in earnest. Her sculpted backside glided before him—down, up, down—stroking him in and out and back into her joyriding goddess body. Her sinuous gilt hair romped about her, rising and falling in dazzling profusion as she pumped on him like a pole-bound carousel Godiva. Dancing, fun-ride curls switched at her flanks, quickening her pace with each descent, the carousel gathering speed. He churned her captive cream hips to explore all of her. He found Annie, then Fanny. He thickened with Mystery Girl and stirred to desire. "Aaaahhh," she cooed, the mirror reflecting her closed eyes and euphoric smile. She matched his gyrations and breathed faster. Her undulating hind end coaxed him. Urged him. Demanded him. Her Siren scent joined in, its vital call egging him toward the brink—Mr. Virility Showpiece, brimming now with purpose. She went at him as if aware of his imminence, of Life's Sweet Mystery itself, her breathing ever faster. The carousel beyond control.

God, but they were good at this! He loved that he could make her pant for it. That her panting made him want to give it. Even when he tried to—

Please, not quite yet.

Her eyes flew open, to a sharp "Oh!" She raised on him and clamped her legs. He peaked and held, capped tight—save for their messy marital marathon. The ever-runny spiral from their syrupy union made way for a glorious rite of passage. Gradually but inexorably her body began to sink … and shove him hotly in. Her clenched wetness forged onto him and inched down, a lengthy, contented "Uuunngghhh" gurgling deep in her throat as she impaled herself with the smearing spiral. A beautiful skewered female submitting in pure bliss, the upshots of conquest coming any splitting second now—Sweet dripping honey dipper, could any man ask for more? She fixed her eyes drunken-like on his, waiting, languid lids adrift upon azure blue. He progressed up through her on his heady pilgrimage, their throbs mingling, swelling, driven to crest as one—an outcome that clamped legs would not deny much longer. His mind reeled and the road seemed to recede. He yanked the car over behind the truck's left taillight and charged down the centerline. This wasn't occasion for a roll in the field.

T HE BRUSQUE SWERVE sped her the rest of the way on, a flurry of honey hair shimmering about her like a golden hue aurora before the gray world outside. He reached for her luminous Eve perfection as for a mirage. Could this pinup girl from paradise actually be his, to pin and pin and pin in that heavenly garden for as long as they both shall live? He brushed through her Adam-luring shimmer to the hot flush of her skin. Traced around her neck, off a shoulder, down her spine. She shied from his touch. Returned, smooth and pliant, to his fingertips. Twisted, bare and yearning, against his palm. She wriggled on him, dangling at his mercy, hands held high by the cheap tin restraints in unconditional Wild West surrender. He seared within her, more invincible with each pitch and turn of her salacious struggle. He soothed along the straining arc of her back, molded his fingers to her heaving ribs, found her pounding like a thoroughbred in a heat for the finish.

Panic-filled pleas escaped her lips, burbled and incoherent, but their meaning clear from the desperation in her eyes. Desperation that seemed wrenched from the ballad that begs him to take her out of pity. He seized her waist and fit his thumb to that special spot low on her back. He pressed. She gasped ... calmed ... followed. He led her to rear up for him one last time and steadied her there. His marvelous stable-kicking mare, poised, postured, and oh-so-very primed for his victory mount. Dazed but radiant, the self-tethered temptress had more than earned her reward—the full extent of it. He ran his hand over her thigh and clasped the lush wellspring of sultry slickness between her legs. She exclaimed in the mirror, her mute image spellbound, mouth open and knowing blue eyes wide.

He glued to the taillights ahead and started her. Emitting a jubilant sob, she parted onto his swollen crown and suckled at it with siphoning ferocity. But it was his turn to toy. He suspended her on his up-thrust staff like a gleaming, hard won trophy—a statuesque beauty meant to be savored. "Please, Danny, please!" she howled. He relished how her raw anguish told him what mattered: He was her male, and he was need-ed. Badly. He made her ask over and over ("Please"), in plaintive wails and imploring body language ("Danny") that, squirm by resolute squirm ("Please"), shinnied him—her steed incarnate bearing his steadfast gift ("Danny"), his teeming siphon ("Please")—deeper, deeper ...

Suddenly, as if spurred to join the action, Ferdie's wayward drive shaft went berserk. "Easy, Big Fellow!" Daniel muttered. *Thrummmmm!*

the shaft quivered. "Ooooo!" Angela squealed. She bore herself straight on. Threw open her legs to take him all. Pleasured him with grinding abandon in the hurtling, devil-may-care night. She made short, urgent sounds, low and muffled, half-joyful, half-beseeching. The sounds became labored, her body glistening … paced him ever faster, her excitement rising with his … grew shrill as they rode one another on sheer instinct. Rode as though tomorrow would never come.

Sweet stud heaven, if ever a little filly deserved—

"Angie!" he called.

She hooked her toes behind his ankles and ponied tight to him, her knuckles white on the overhead restraint. The brute shaft below tremored with the might of its pent-up reserve. "Yes!" she choked. Her huge eyes searching back said the rest.

Those eyes would get her everything. Letting all else go, he clung to the blur of the highway stripes. Rushing in. Growing solid. Unstoppable.

Why him? Any man she wanted would have given anything for this, any time. But this ravishing creature wanted him, here and—

—now.

His foot lurched on the throttle and the shaft coupled headlong. He wielded his vehicle with a coursing thrill, the unchecked forces surging upward. Angela jerked back and cried out, staring with that ripe-and-ready wonder, and wondering, that makes a man be extra thorough. She drove herself on him. Slipped and slued and writhed on his lap. Thrashed her head every which way, the frantic reception that always so gratified him … and guaranteed the five-legged stamina to keep her hair happily in the air. Her fun-flung honey mane flayed at their lathered bareness— relentless Lady LaRue floggings, each exquisite lash landing cool against skin cloaked in nothing but the sybaritic sheen of arousal and aerobics. The damp swats, spanks, and smacks inflicted by her kinky silk ringlets masqueraded as gentle reprimands, all the while whipping them both into an unbridled frenzy. Ferdie shook from the bone-jarring spasms of its burrowing shaft, and Angela rammed in Man o'War. Rammed him in like never before, hair soaring and eyes wild, a filly on fire with the firm sureness of her destiny. Again and again her bucking, love-glazed body sheathed him to the hilt, fast and hard, each time with a hoarse, guttural utterance that confirmed her fever to sheath him yet again.

"Unh! My stallion! Unh!" she plunged and pleaded, "Fill me!"

And—as he did—he rejoiced from the very core of his being. To have and to hold, to have and to love, to have and to mate. His angel of the morning, noon, and night.

She was real!

DEAR READER

Enjoy the story?

• Please give an online review wherever you bought this book.

• And please pass the word—send kindred spirits to

www.OverdrivePress.com

Thanks!

Danny O

DANNY O'TOOLE writes and plays guitar with Angela in Minnesota. Their vehicle still has overdrive.

FOR THE WRITER IN YOU

Have your own stirring story to tell? Put those "penned up" desires straight (or what have you) to bed! Learn from the author how to sweet-talk your way from A to X in your own stimulating prose.

• Aspiring fiction writers, make the seductive leap from nonfiction— and spice up your life doing it!

• Repressed fiction writers, portray all the thrills your characters have coming—between the lines and on the sheets!

Among the writing approaches exemplified in "Honeymoon In Overdrive" are two extremes, each tailored to serve plot and character development:

(1) The wedding night's three steamy acts, highlighted in just 100 quickie words.

(2) The symbolic following night of, um, mounting action, savored in 5,000 tell-all words.

Develop your own tale with just the right amount of tail. Learn from these and other examples how to perk up your writing at

www.WriteYourSexyStory.com

ACKNOWLEDGMENTS

My muse
My merrymaker
My master booksmith

My love 'til the end of time.

WAIT, THERE'S MORE!

If you missed the Sixties (bummer, man) chances are you also missed a few of this story's spazzed-out *bons mots*. For openers, did you dig all sixty-one highway hits that revisit the groovy days of the Crown Vic's Town and Country radio?

Keep on chooglin'—boogie to the outta sight tunes, hip toys, and other far out blasts at

www.OverdrivePress.com

Be there or be square.

PHOTO ALBUM

Here are a few of Danny's favorite snapshots. As he comes across others, he'll add them to further your enjoyment at

www.OverdrivePress.com

...where you will also find links to the e-book version with color photos!

DANNY O'TOOLE

The author reflects on Angela's 1928 National slide guitar, her "Janey Winter Special."

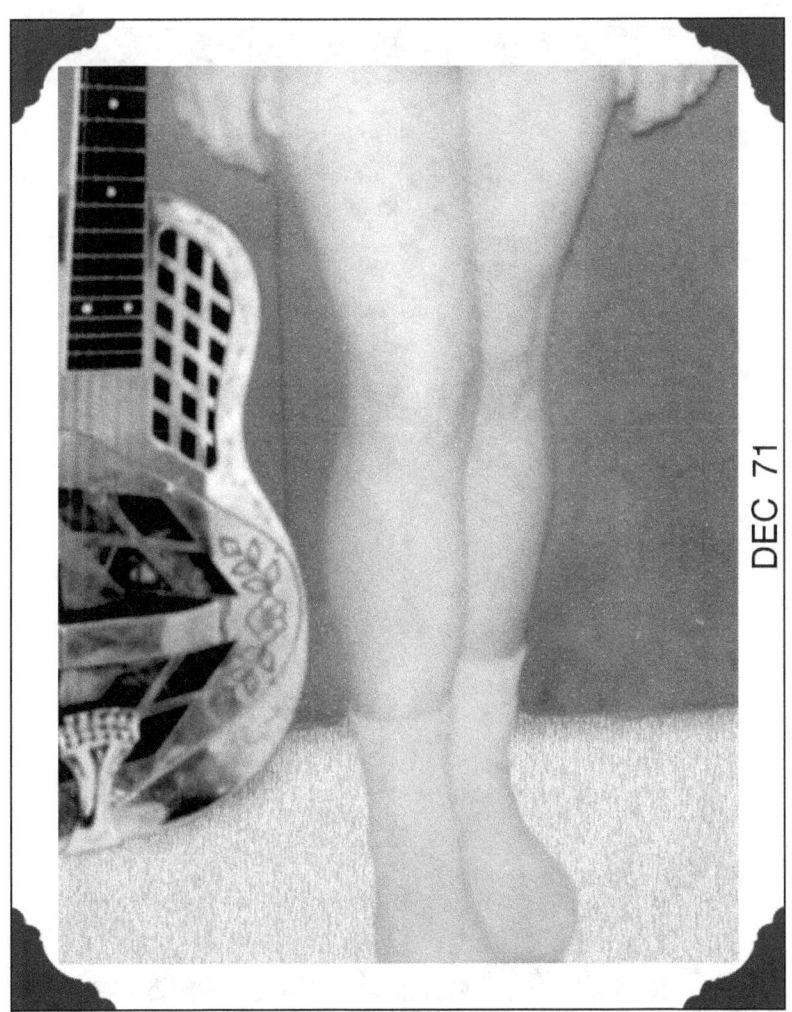

DEC 71

NORTH COUNTRY FARE

Hot Dish Angela, served up to drive a guy loony.

FEB 69

PULLING INTO NAZARETH

1943 D-18 Dreadnaught with 1968 O-16NY New Yorker. Oh, the magic of Martins!

DEC 71

CASE STUDY

Nomadic Warrior and Flower Child Bride.

THE *COUP DE L'AMOUR*

Bookmarks of a fairytale romance.

THE HOLLEY TRINITY

How you feed two hundred ravenous horses.

DEC 71

PULLING INTO THE BIG APPLE

By George, we made it!

DEC 71

HANG ONTO YOUR HAT...

... THE HONEYMOON HAS JUST BEGUN!

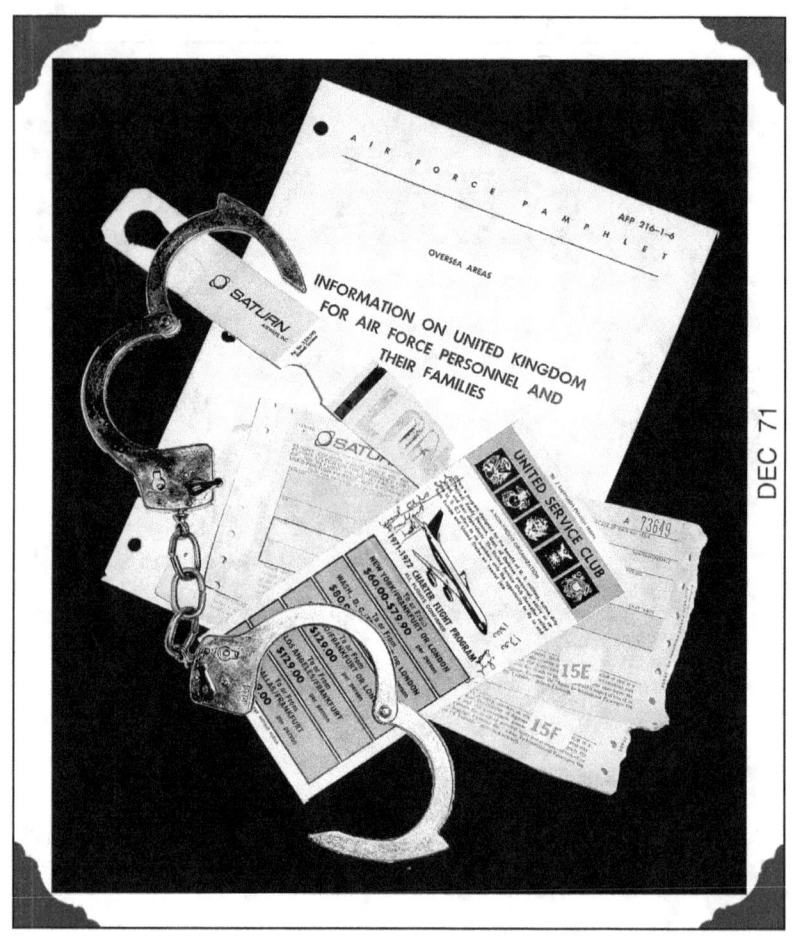

See what's in store at
www.OverdrivePress.com

www.ingramcontent.com/pod-product-compliance
Lightning Source LLC
Chambersburg PA
CBHW071216130626
46555CB00004B/1733